Snowed in Love

SHANI DENISE

 Formatted with Vellum

About the Author

Shani Denise writes soulful, spicy urban romances that celebrate Black love in all its beauty, power, and magic. A proud Detroit native, she infuses every story with the city's signature blend of grit and warmth. Penned the poetic lover girl, Shani brings a lyrical boldness to her storytelling—her voice raw, heartfelt, and unapologetically real. Through richly drawn characters and emotional, heat-filled narratives, she delivers love, healing, and intensity on every page, crafting unforgettable stories that linger long after the last chapter.

CHAPTER 1
Snowed In on I-94

THE SNOW CAME DOWN like handfuls of feathers tossed from the heavens, covering everything in sight with a thick, icy blanket. Streetlights blurred into golden halos through the whiteout, and the hum of the freeway was replaced by the angry hiss of tires losing grip on black ice. Jasmine Carter gripped her steering wheel tighter, heart pounding as her silver sedan shuddered to a stop on the shoulder of I-94. Her windshield wipers fought for their life, squeaking across glass buried under snow.

"Come on, not tonight," she whispered, her breath fogging the air. She had just left work late from the hospital, and all she wanted was to get home to her tiny apartment in Midtown, light a candle, and sip cocoa. Instead, she was stuck in the kind of storm that made the city stop breathing. When she saw the flicker of headlights approaching in her rearview mirror, she prayed it wasn't trouble. The vehicle loomed larger, a massive black Ford F-350, its lights cutting through the storm like search beams. It slowed, tires crunching over snow and ice, and came to a stop behind her.

Jasmine's pulse jumped.

"Oh no... nope, I read too much for this," she muttered,

locking her doors and reaching for pinky her pink .38 in the middle console just as a tall figure stepped out, bundled in a thick parka and hat.

A deep voice called over the wind.

"Hey! You okay in there? Looks like you're stuck!"

She cracked the window an inch, snow swirling inside. "I'm fine, thanks!" she shouted. "My brother's on the way." (A lie — her brother lived in Atlanta.)

He tilted his head, a faint smile on his lips. "Ma'am, no disrespect, but there's no way your brother's making it through this storm. Let me help you out. My mom would kill me if I left somebody out here freezing."

That simple line, genuine and laced with warmth made her hesitate and place pinky back. There was something in his tone that didn't sound like danger. It sounded like home.

Jasmine studied him through the cracked window. The snowflakes clung to his lashes and beard, the streetlight catching on the warmth of his dark brown skin. His breath came out in steady clouds, calm in the chaos swirling all around them.

Her fingers hovered over the lock button. Every voice of reason told her not to open that door but then the wind howled, rocking the car, and the temperature on her dashboard blinked 10°.

She sighed, her teeth chattering.

"You said your mom would kill you if you left me out here?"

He grinned, rubbing his hands together. "Absolutely. She raised me better than that. I'm Marcus, by the way. Promise I'm not a serial killer, just a man with a shovel and a tow strap."

That made her laugh despite herself. "I'm Jasmine."

"Nice to meet you, Jasmine. Let's get you outta this snowbank before you turn into a popsicle."

He opened her door carefully, shielding her from the

blowing snow with his arm like a human barrier. The blast of icy wind hit her face, and she gasped, noticing how he moved to block the wind with ease, like he'd done this before.

"Hop in my truck," he said gently opening the door to usher her in. "I'll see if she starts."

Normally, she'd say no. But something about the way he said it, steady, respectful, not pushy but authoritative, made her trust him.

Within minutes, she was sitting in the passenger seat of his F-350, the heater humming like heaven, the smell of leather and cedar wrapping around her.

He stomped snow off his boots and slid in beside her, shaking his head with a grin.

"Detroit winters don't play fair. I should've guessed I'd find somebody stranded tonight."

"Guess I'm lucky you did," she said softly, rubbing her hands in front of the vents.

For a moment, they just sat there two strangers in a blizzard, listening to the quiet hum of the storm outside. And somewhere between the snowflakes and the warmth, something unspoken settled between them.

It wasn't just relief. It was connection.

Marcus leaned back in his seat, rubbing his palms together in front of the heat vents. "Man, this truck's working overtime tonight," he said with a chuckle. Then he turned toward her, his tone softening. "You get a hold of your brother yet?"

Jasmine hesitated, eyes dropping to the phone glowing dimly in her hand. The signal bar mocked her with a single, flickering line.

She exhaled, embarrassed. "So... about that. My brother's in Atlanta."

Marcus raised an eyebrow, a smile tugging at his lips. "Atlanta, huh? That's a long drive in a snowstorm."

She laughed a little, covering her face. "I know, I know. I

panicked. You pulled up out of nowhere, and all I could think about was every scary book or movie I've ever watched."

"Fair," he said, nodding. "If I saw a big dude in a truck pulling up behind me in the middle of a blizzard, I might lie too."

That made her relax. His easy humor melted the tension she'd been holding since her car stopped moving.

"I'm sorry," she said quietly. "I didn't mean to lie. I just didn't know what else to say."

"No harm done," Marcus replied. "You were trying to stay safe. Smart woman."

For a moment, silence filled the truck again, but it wasn't awkward. The kind of silence that felt calm. Safe. The kind she hadn't felt in a long time.

He glanced at her again, his deep voice warm over the sound of the heater. "Tell you what, Jasmine-without-a-brother-nearby, you stay in here, stay warm, and I'll see if I can dig you out and get you back on the road. Deal?"

She smiled, finally letting go of the fear that had been gripping her. "Deal. But please be careful out there."

He gave her a little salute and opened the door, a gust of snow rushing in before it shut again. Jasmine watched through the windshield as Marcus disappeared into the flurry, a dark silhouette moving against a white sky and for the first time all night, she didn't feel stranded.

She felt seen.

Through the thick curtain of snow, Jasmine could barely make out Marcus's figure as he worked. His truck headlights cast long beams through the blizzard, catching him in flashes. The broad set of his shoulders, the strength in his movements as he tried to dig her car's tires free.

The temperature on his dashboard blinked 0° now, and she could feel the chill creeping even inside the truck. The snow was coming harder, faster and swallowing the freeway whole.

When Marcus bent down to scoop more snow, she caught herself staring. Even buried under layers of winter gear, he had that kind of build that said he could move mountains or at least a snowbank or two. The kind of man who looked capable and calm no matter how bad things got.

But this storm was no joke.

She leaned forward and pressed the horn, just one long, sharp honk that echoed into the frozen air.

He turned immediately, his face barely visible through the flurries. She motioned for him to come back.

Marcus jogged to the driver's side, snow clinging to his coat and hat. When he opened the door, a blast of freezing air rushed in with him.

"What's wrong?" he asked, breathing hard, his cheeks dusted white.

Jasmine shook her head. "Marcus, I appreciate you trying, really, but I don't think it's safe to stay out here. The temperature just dropped again. This storm is getting worse by the minute."

He looked back toward her stranded car, snow already halfway up the doors. "Yeah," he said after a beat, "you're probably right. Even the tow trucks will take hours in this mess."

"I can call AAA and have them get my car later," she said, rubbing her hands for warmth. Then, hesitantly, she added, "Would you mind dropping me off somewhere safe? Maybe a gas station or... anywhere with heat?"

He turned to her, a small frown tugging at his lips despite the cold.

"Jasmine, I'm not about to drop you at some gas station. My mom's house is about fifteen minutes from here, and she's the kind who keeps hot cocoa ready for emergencies. You'll be warmer there while we wait this out."

She blinked, surprised. "Your mom's house? You sure she won't mind? I can call a friend once we get there."

He chuckled, brushing snow off his coat. "She'd probably fuss at me if I didn't bring you. Trust me, she lives for these Hallmark moments." That made her laugh, easing the tension in her chest. Maybe it was the exhaustion, or the warmth finally creeping back into her fingers, but she felt something else too, comfort.

"Okay," she said softly. "I'll take that ride."

Marcus grinned, started the truck, and turned the heater up. As they pulled away from her half-buried car, the snow swallowed their tire tracks behind them — two strangers carried through the storm toward something neither of them expected. The truck rumbled down the nearly invisible stretch of I-94, its headlights fighting through the thick swirl of snow. Inside, it was warm, a cocoon of humming heat, low music from the radio, and the faint scent of cedar and leather that seemed to follow Marcus.

Jasmine sat quietly at first, watching the world blur white through her window. Her body finally relaxed now that she was out of danger, but her mind was still catching up to the fact that she was in a stranger's truck, a stranger who, against all odds, made her feel safe.

"So," Marcus said, glancing over with a small grin, "You from around here, Jasmine-with-the-Atlanta-brother?"

She laughed softly, shaking her head. "Born and raised on the east side. Grew up near Jefferson and Lakewood, right by the water. You?"

"West side. Grand River area," he said proudly, tapping the steering wheel. "We'd probably argue over which coney spot's better."

"Oh, that's easy — Lafayette's."

He shot her a look of mock offense. "You mean American. Don't do that to me now!"

Their laughter filled the truck, warming the air even more than the heater.

A few miles later, the laughter faded into an easy quiet, the kind that felt like they'd known each other longer than thirty minutes.

"So, what do you do, and why are you out in one of the worst snowstorms?" he asked, glancing over as the wipers squeaked across the windshield.

"I'm a nurse," she said. "ER. Henry Ford Hospital. Long shifts, lots of caffeine, and not enough sleep. I just got off work before the storm hit."

His brow lifted. "Your serious? ER nurse? That explains the calm under pressure. Most folks would've been crying in that car by now."

She smiled faintly. "Oh, I was panicking. I just hide it well."

He nodded, impressed. "That's real, though. My sister's a travel nurse. I don't know how y'all do it? All those long nights, seeing what you see, and still showing up every day. Takes heart."

Jasmine glanced at him, touched by the sincerity in his voice. "Thanks. What about you? You seem like the type that's good with your hands and I'm not just talking about with a shovel."

He grinned. "Depends but you're not wrong. I'm an engineer at Ford. Working mostly on powertrain systems. Been there about eight years now."

Her eyes widened. "Ford engineer? That's impressive."

He shrugged modestly. "It pays the bills. My dad worked there, too. Guess it's in the blood."

Something about the way he said that made her smile — there was pride in his voice, but also humility. The kind that came from hard work, not ego.

"Detroit through and through," she said.

"You know it." He glanced her way again, that grin tugging at his lips. "And you — a nurse out here saving lives. I think we make a pretty solid snowstorm duo."

She laughed, shaking her head. "You're ridiculous."

“Maybe,” he said, turning down a quiet, snow-covered street lined with glowing holiday lights. “But you’re smiling, so I’ll take it.”

For a brief moment, the storm outside didn’t feel so fierce. Between the hum of the heater and the low hum of his voice, Jasmine felt something she hadn’t expected to find on the side of I-94. Peace.

CHAPTER 2

Snowbound Comfort

MARCUS TURNED off the main road and onto a quiet neighborhood street lined with tall, snow-covered trees and glowing porch lights. The storm still raged, but here the world seemed softer, every house outlined in twinkling Christmas bulbs, and snowflakes glittering in the glow of it all.

"This your mom's block?" Jasmine asked, peering out the window.

"Yeah," he said, smiling as he slowed the truck. "She's been here forever. Don't let her fool you, though — she'll act like this storm's the perfect excuse to feed you like you haven't eaten in a week."

Jasmine chuckled. "After tonight, I might not even argue."

They pulled into the driveway of a cozy brick house trimmed in gold lights and crowned with a giant lit-up angel in the yard. The warmth of the scene was almost enough to make her forget how cold it was outside. Marcus hopped out first, jogging around to her side. "Wait right there. Ice gets slick over here." When he opened the door, the wind nipped at their faces again. He offered his hand without hesitation. Jasmine hesitated only for a second before taking it, his grip was steady, strong, and reassuring.

The front door opened before they even reached it.

"Marcus Darnell Johnson! You better have a good reason for being out in this storm and about to track half of Detroit's snow into my foyer!"

A woman's voice, rich and warm like Sunday morning coffee, called out from the doorway.

Marcus laughed under his breath. "Told you," He whispered to Jasmine before calling out, "Ma, calm down! I brought company!"

"Company?" The woman stepped forward, wrapped in a red housecoat, her silver hair pinned neatly. When she saw Jasmine, her expression softened immediately. "Oh, baby, come in here! You must be freezing!"

Before Jasmine could even respond, Marcus's mom had ushered her inside, stripping off her coat and thrusting a pair of fuzzy slippers at her feet. The smell of cinnamon, cocoa, and something sweet, filled the house.

"I'm Mrs. Johnson," she said. "And you are?"

"Jasmine," she replied, shy but smiling. "Thank you for letting me come in. The storm got bad out there."

"Oh, honey, you don't have to thank me," Mrs. Johnson said, waving a hand. "You're safe now. Sit down, warm up. Marcus, hang this girl's coat up and fix her a cup of cocoa."

"Yes, ma'am," he said, smirking as he hung both their coats near the door.

Jasmine sank into the plush sofa, the glow from the Christmas tree reflecting in her eyes. She couldn't remember the last time she'd been in a house that felt this full of warmth.

"So," Mrs. Johnson said, sitting beside her, "how'd my son end up with you in this blizzard?"

Jasmine smiled, glancing toward Marcus as he stirred cocoa in the kitchen. "I got stuck on I-94 after work. He stopped to help, even when I told him not to."

Mrs. Johnson chuckled. "That sounds like him. His daddy

used to do the same thing, couldn't drive past a stranded soul if he tried."

Marcus returned with two steaming mugs, handing one to Jasmine. "Don't let her fool you. She's the reason I stopped. She would've shown up in my dreams tonight if I didn't."

"You're right about that," his mom said with a grin.

They all laughed, the sound blending with the faint hum of Donny Hathaway's This Christmas playing on the radio. Jasmine sipped her cocoa, warmth spreading through her chest.

For the first time in a long while, she wasn't thinking about work, deadlines, or exhaustion. Just this — the lights, the laughter, the feeling of belonging in a stranger's living room on a snowy Detroit night.

Marcus met her gaze from across the coffee table. "See?" he said softly. "Told you she'd have cocoa ready."

Jasmine smiled over the rim of her mug. "Guess you were right."

And in that cozy room filled with the scent of sugar and spice, something new began to bloom in the quiet. It was steady, and full of promise.

The wind howled outside, rattling the windows like it was trying to come in. Snow danced under the streetlights in wild spirals, piling higher and higher against the porch.

Mrs. Johnson peeked out the window, shaking her head. "Lord have mercy, that storm's not letting up one bit. You two aren't going anywhere tonight."

Jasmine looked up from her cocoa. "Oh, I don't want to intrude. I can call an Uber—"

Marcus and his mother said it at the same time.

"An Uber?"

Mrs. Johnson turned to her with that firm, motherly look that needed no words. "Baby, I love your spirit, but no Uber driver in his right mind is out in this mess. You see that snow? You'll be lucky if a plow even passes through before morning."

Jasmine gave a sheepish smile. "Guess I hadn't thought about that."

"Well, you'll think about it after a hot meal," Mrs. Johnson said, already heading toward the kitchen. "Marcus, set the table. I made pot roast earlier and there's mac and cheese in the oven. Lord knew somebody was gonna need feeding tonight."

Marcus grinned. "She's serious about feeding people, Jasmine. You might leave here with leftovers and a new church home."

Jasmine laughed, following him into the kitchen. The house smelled like heaven, roasted meat, butter, and cornbread. The kind of aroma that wrapped itself around you and said you're safe now.

As they sat down, Mrs. Johnson loaded their plates like a woman on a mission. "Y'all eat," she insisted. "Can't nobody face a blizzard on an empty stomach."

The conversation flowed easily. Marcus told funny stories from his job at the plant and how the guys would bet on who could build an engine part the fastest, or how one coworker accidentally set off the assembly alarm by dancing too close to a sensor. Jasmine laughed until her side hurt.

Then Mrs. Johnson turned to Jasmine. "So, baby, you said you're a nurse? Bless your heart. That's God's work right there. Did Marcus tell you his sister is a travel nurse? She wanted to see the world and she's doing it!"

Jasmine nodded humbly. Sometimes, it's tough, but I love helping people. I guess I'm wired for chaos."

Marcus chuckled. "Explains how you handled being stranded on I-94 like a champ."

She smiled. "I was panicking, trust me. Just didn't want you to see it."

Mrs. Johnson smiled knowingly. "You two sound like you've known each other longer than a few hours."

Jasmine's cheeks warmed. Marcus glanced her way, his eyes

soft but amused. "Maybe the storm just sped things up," he said quietly.

Dinner stretched into easy laughter and second helpings. Outside, the storm roared like an ocean, but inside the Johnson house, warmth ruled.

Later, Jasmine tried again to leave. She slipped away to the window, phone in hand, checking for a signal. Nothing. Not even one bar. She opened her ride app, but the screen flashed: No drivers available.

Marcus came up beside her, hands in his pockets. "Told you, he said, voice low. "Even the tow trucks gave up hours ago."

She sighed. "I hate feeling like a burden."

He shook his head. "You're not. My mom's probably praying for more reasons to fuss over someone. You're doing her a favor."

From the kitchen, Mrs. Johnson called out, "What y'all whispering about? The guest room's ready! Jasmine, you're staying put until that snow stops."

Jasmine turned, wide-eyed. "Oh, I couldn't"

"Hush, girl," Mrs. Johnson said with a wave of her hand. "You're family now. My son doesn't bring just anybody through my door. Now come get yourself a blanket before I lose my patience."

Jasmine exchanged a smile with Marcus. "Does she always get her way?"

He grinned. "Pretty much."

As Mrs. Johnson fussed over extra pillows and peppermint tea, Jasmine realized something strange — for the first time all night, she didn't feel stranded. She felt like she belonged.

Outside, the storm raged on, burying Detroit in white. Inside, the lights glowed soft and golden, and a new kind of warmth began to take root between two souls who'd found each other by chance on a freezing highway.

Jasmine stood in the small, cozy guest room, the scent of

lavender and fresh linen wrapping around her like comfort itself. Mrs. Johnson had insisted she take a hot shower and left a neatly folded set of flannel pajamas on the bed — red-and-black plaid, soft and warm.

"They were for my daughter, but she's not coming home this Christmas staying local with her friends, so she doesn't get caught in this storm like you I guess or stuck for a week like the last time she came home," Mrs. Johnson said laughing and shrugging her shoulders. "Never been worn. You'll sleep better in something cozy."

Now, with her hair pulled into a loose bun and her skin warm from the shower, Jasmine slipped into the pajamas. They were a little big but soft against her skin, making her feel safe, tucked away from the chaos outside.

She glanced toward the window the snow still falling in thick, endless sheets, the world outside swallowed by white. The clock on the nightstand glowed 12:07 a.m., the house quiet except for the faint hum of the furnace.

Then came the knock.

Soft at first. Then again, two slow taps.

Her heart skipped. She froze, listening.

Another knock. "Jasmine? It's Marcus."

His deep voice rumbled through the door, calm but concerned.

She opened it halfway, startled and a little self-conscious. He stood there barefoot, wearing an A-shirt and the same flannel pajama pants, probably another set from his mother's stash. His skin glowed a deep bronze under the hallway light, muscles defined and relaxed at once, like he'd just walked out of a dream.

"Hey," he said softly, giving her that easy smile that warmed the coldest corners of her heart. "Sorry to bother you. I just wanted to make sure you were good. My mom worries, and well, I guess I do too."

Jasmine tried to speak, but for a second all she could do

was look. The way his shoulders filled out his shirt, the calm confidence in his posture, and those warm brown eyes, kind, steady, and focused only on her.

She swallowed hard, willing her voice to come back. "I—yeah, I'm fine. Just getting settled. Your mom's a sweetheart."

He leaned against the doorframe, arms folded, a playful smirk on his lips. "Told you she'd adopt you in about an hour. You should've seen her earlier, she already said you're coming for Christmas dinner."

Jasmine laughed softly, shaking her head. "She's something else."

"Yeah," he said, smiling, his voice lowering just a little. "She's got a heart too big for this world."

For a brief moment, silence filled the space between them again, not awkward, but electric. The storm outside howled, wind brushing against the windows like it was trying to remind them how cold the world could be. But here, in this warm little corner of the house, everything felt still.

"Are you really okay?" he asked again, his tone gentle now. "I know today has been a lot with the storm and being stuck with strangers."

She met his gaze. "I don't feel like I'm with strangers anymore."

He smiled, slow and genuine, the kind that reached his eyes. "Good. Get some rest, Jasmine."

"You too, Marcus."

He gave a small nod, backing away from the doorway. But before he turned down the hall, he paused, his voice low and smooth. "And for what it's worth — you look good in plaid."

Jasmine's breath caught, her cheeks heating despite the cold draft from the window.

When she closed the door and leaned against it, she couldn't help but smile. Outside, the blizzard roared. Inside, something else entirely was beginning to stir quietly, unexpected, and impossible to ignore.

CHAPTER 3

Morning After the Storm

WHEN JASMINE OPENED HER EYES, the first thing she noticed was the silence.

The world outside was still, no more wind, no more rattling windows, no sound but the soft ticking of the clock on the wall. For a second, she forgot where she was. The scent of coffee drifting down the hall reminded her. Mrs. Johnson's guest room was bathed in a golden light now. The storm had finally passed. She stretched, the flannel warm against her skin, and padded quietly to the window. The entire block was blanketed in white, rooftops shimmering under the morning sun. Even the street looked like it had been dipped in sugar. She smiled to herself. Detroit hadn't looked this peaceful in years.

Pulling her robe tighter, she stepped into the hallway, following the sound of faint old-school R&B, playing soft and low. In the kitchen, she found Marcus standing by the stove, back turned, wearing a white T-shirt and gray sweats. He was humming along to "This Christmas" as he flipped pancakes with a practiced ease. For a second, she just watched him. The morning light caught the curve of his shoulders, the easy rhythm of his movements. There was something steady about him, that quiet kind of man who made chaos feel nonexistent. He turned, catching her in the doorway.

"Well, good morning, sleepyhead," he said with a grin. "Hope you're hungry."

Jasmine smiled shyly. "I am now. You cook too?"

"Engineer by trade, breakfast chef by survival," he teased. "My mom's still asleep, so I figured I'd handle breakfast duty."

She moved closer, the smell of butter and maple syrup making her stomach growl. "I could've helped."

He raised a brow. "Oh? You any good in the kitchen?"

"I can hold my own," she said playfully. "Hospital cafeterias don't exactly inspire gourmet skills, but I manage."

He chuckled, sliding a plate of golden pancakes her way. "Well, Nurse Jasmine, consider this your morning prescription: carbs, caffeine, and a side of recovery."

She laughed, taking a seat at the small kitchen table. "You're ridiculous."

"Yeah, but you're smiling again, so I'll take that as a win."

They ate in easy silence for a moment, the comfort between them deepening with every small glance, every quiet laugh.

"So," he said after a while, sipping his coffee, "what's next for you once the roads clear up?"

She hesitated, swirling syrup on her plate. "Back to the hustle and bustle, I guess. We've been short-staffed since Thanksgiving, and the holidays make everything busier."

He nodded. "I get that. I'll be back at the plant too. New model's in testing, so long hours, lots of pressure. Sometimes I wonder if I'll ever stop working long enough to live."

Jasmine looked up at him, surprised by the vulnerability in his tone. "That's exactly how I feel," she admitted. "Like life's just... on autopilot. Work, sleep, repeat."

Their eyes met — steady, searching, unguarded.

Marcus set down his cup, leaning forward slightly. "Maybe

that's why storms happen sometimes. To make us stop. To make us notice what we've been missing." She didn't reply right away, but her heart did. It beat faster, louder, as if agreeing with every word he said.

Mrs. Johnson's voice suddenly called from the hallway, breaking the spell.

"Lord have mercy, y'all up already? I was coming to make breakfast!"

Marcus grinned, calling back, "Already handled, Ma!"

Mrs. Johnson appeared, smiling when she saw Jasmine at the table. "Mmm-hmm, I see that. Pancakes and smiles that's how you know a storm done some good."

Jasmine blushed. "Morning, Mrs. Johnson."

"Morning, baby," she said warmly. "You stay as long as you need, all right? Ain't no rush. Roads are probably still frozen solid." Jasmine nodded, grateful. But as she looked out the frosted kitchen window and then back at Marcus — at the warmth in his eyes, at the quiet promise in his smile — she couldn't help but wonder if maybe fate had its own plans for her morning after the storm.

By late afternoon, the city was slowly coming back to life. The plows had finally made it down the block, carving narrow lanes through the mountains of snow. The sky was still pale and hazy, but streaks of sunlight glimmered across the icy rooftops. Jasmine stood at the window, cradling a mug of tea Mrs. Johnson had made for her, peppermint with a dash of honey. The house smelled like vanilla candles and fresh laundry. It felt like peace. Behind her, Marcus walked in, pulling on his boots. "Roads are still slick, but they cleared the freeway enough to check on your car," he said. "You up for a little adventure?"

She turned, smiling. "You're seriously going out there already?"

He shrugged with a grin. "Well, I can't let your car freeze

out there forever. Plus, I'm curious if she's still got some fight left in her."

Mrs. Johnson appeared in the doorway, hands on her hips. "You two be careful out there. And Marcus take my emergency blanket and that extra shovel in the garage. I don't want to see you both on Channel 4 news saying my child's stranded."

Marcus laughed. "Yes, ma'am."

Jasmine bundled up in her borrowed coat and scarf, feeling oddly content. The cold air hit her cheeks as they stepped outside, but it wasn't unpleasant, it was refreshing, clean, and new. The streets were quiet except for the distant hum of plows. The snow crunched under their boots as they walked to the truck. Marcus opened the door for her again, that small gesture not going unnoticed. She slid in, cheeks flushed from the cold or maybe something else. The drive was slow, the world around them glistening like a postcard. As they approached the freeway ramp, the aftermath of the blizzard showed itself: cars half-buried, exits closed, snowdrifts piled high against the guardrails.

"Wow," Jasmine murmured. "It's like the whole city hit pause."

"Detroit's tough," Marcus said, eyes scanning the road. "She slows down, but she never stops. Kinda like you."

She laughed softly. "You don't even know me well enough to say that."

He glanced over, a teasing smile tugging at his lips. "I know enough. You were stuck in zero degrees and still trying to lie your way out of help. That's Detroit spirit if I've ever seen it."

Jasmine rolled her eyes but couldn't hide her grin. "Okay, maybe you have a point."

They finally spotted her car, half-buried near the shoulder where she'd left it. Marcus parked and hopped out first, trudging through the snow with his shovel. Together they brushed off the hood, laughing each time a gust of wind blew snow back into their faces. When they finally got the door open, Jasmine tried the ignition. It sputtered weakly, then died. "Looks like she's not waking up anytime soon," she sighed.

Marcus tapped the roof lightly. "We'll get her towed tomorrow. You just made it out of a blizzard alive — that's a win."

She smiled, leaning back in the seat. "You're good at this."

"At what?" Marcus replied.

"Showing up," she said softly. "You didn't even know me, and you showed up right on time."

His expression softened, eyes meeting hers in the quiet of the truck. "Maybe I was supposed to."

For a moment, the world seemed to still again no wind, no noise, just the soft hum of something neither of them could quite name. When they pulled back into his mom's driveway later, Mrs. Johnson already had dinner warming in the oven, baked chicken, rice, and collard greens. "See? Knew y'all would be hungry again," she said proudly, ushering them inside. After dinner, Jasmine helped clear the table, still laughing at Mrs. Johnson's stories about Marcus's childhood. Every now and then, she caught Marcus looking at her, not in a bold way, but with quiet admiration, like he was trying to figure out how someone could walk into a snowstorm and somehow make the whole house warmer. When she finally reached for her coat, phone in hand, she hesitated. "Looks like the city is back open now. I should probably head out soon."

Mrs. Johnson frowned. "You sure, baby? It's still slick out there."

Before Jasmine could answer, Marcus spoke up, his voice easy but firm. "Or you could come back tomorrow. We're doing our annual Christmas Eve dinner, family, friends, and a lot of food. You'd fit right in."

Jasmine blinked, surprised. "You want me to come back?"

Mrs. Johnson nodded before Marcus could even answer. "Absolutely. I'll even save you a seat next to my son."

Jasmine laughed, glancing at Marcus. "Sounds like I don't have a choice."

Marcus smiled that slow, magnetic grin that seemed to melt the last bit of winter in the air. "You always got a choice, Jasmine. But I'd like it if you said yes."

Her heart fluttered as she met his gaze. "Then yes," she said softly.

Outside, the snow began to fall again light this time, and gentle as if the city itself approved. And for the first time, Jasmine didn't dread being snowed in. Because maybe, just maybe, this storm had led her exactly where she was meant to be. By evening, the world outside glowed again not from the storm this time, but from the soft halo of streetlights bouncing off the snow. The roads were somewhat clear, and the city was still slowly waking up from its whiteout slumber. Jasmine stood by the front door, coat zipped, boots on, phone in hand.

"My friend Starr just texted me," she said to Marcus and his mom. "She got off her shift at the hospital early and she's not far from here. She offered to swing by and take me home."

Mrs. Johnson pursed her lips. "You sure you don't want to stay another night or have Marcus take you? Roads might still be slick."

"I'll be okay, I promise," Jasmine said with a grateful smile. "You've both done more than enough for me. But I will be back for Christmas Eve dinner, you have my word."

Mrs. Johnson's expression softened instantly. "All right, baby. I'll hold you to that. And you better come hungry."

"Oh, I will," Jasmine laughed.

Marcus grabbed his coat. "I'll walk you out.

I'll make sure she gets to the car safely, Ma."

Outside, the evening was still and bright. The snow

crunched beneath their boots as they walked to the curb, the air crisp and cool. A few houses down, headlights appeared a dark SUV pulling up slowly before stopping in front of them.

"That's her," Jasmine said, waving.

The passenger window rolled down, and a woman with long braids and a knowing smile leaned out. "You must be Marcus," she said, her tone half-teasing. "The snow hero?"

Marcus chuckled. "Something like that."

"Mm-hmm," Starr hummed, eyes glinting. "Well, I appreciate you taking care of my girl."

"Anytime," Marcus replied, opening the passenger door for Jasmine. "You sure you'll be good?"

Jasmine nodded, her breath visible in the cold. "Yeah. Thank you again, Marcus. For everything."

He smiled, that quiet, grounding smile she'd come to recognize. "Just glad you're safe. See you soon?"

She hesitated for only a second before saying softly, "Yeah. See you soon."

For a heartbeat, neither of them moved. The world felt suspended — the crisp air between them carrying a spark neither could quite name. Then Jasmine climbed into the SUV, and Marcus closed the door gently, giving a small wave as they pulled away.

Starr didn't even wait until they hit the next block. "Okay," she said, turning down the music. "Start talking. Now. Baby that Man is Fine, Fine He can save me anytime, shoot I think my tire need some air in it right now."

Jasmine laughed, covering her face. "It's not even like that, and believe me I noticed how fine he is, but he was just being nice."

"The man walked you to the car and opened the door like he didn't want you to leave. Friend it is exactly like that," Starr shot back. And the way y'all were looking at each other? Girl, that wasn't just weather-friendly behavior." Now spill it!"

Jasmine sighed, smiling despite herself. "Fine. I got stuck

on I-94 last night. He stopped to help, and it turned into this whole thing — his mom took me in during the storm. They fed me, made me cocoa, gave me pajamas, the whole nine."

Starr gasped dramatically. "Pajamas? Oh, that's intimate hospitality!"

"Not like that," Jasmine said quickly, laughing. "His mom's amazing. And Marcus—" pausing, her tone softening — "he's just... different. Kind. Real."

Starr glanced at her sideways, grinning. "And fine?"

"Very," Jasmine admitted with a laugh. "Tall, dark, gorgeous. Works at Ford, smart, easygoing. It's crazy I've known him less than a day and I can't stop thinking about him even now."

Starr snapped her fingers. "Mm-hmm. That's chemistry, baby. You going to that Christmas Eve dinner?"

"Absolutely."

"Good. Then you betta wear something festive and fitted. Something that hugs them curves, because you, my friend, are about to make that man forget about the weather forecast."

Jasmine laughed so hard she nearly dropped her phone. "You're terrible."

"I'm right, though." said Starr.

By the time Starr pulled up to Jasmine's apartment building, the laughter had eased into quiet smiles. The snow sparkled under the city lights, soft and magical. Inside her apartment, Jasmine kicked off her boots and leaned against the door, exhaling deeply. The stillness felt too quiet now, too empty. Her mind drifted right back to Marcus — his smile, his warmth, the way his voice had sounded when he said see you soon. She wandered to her closet, pulling out hangers and rifling through her clothes. "Something festive and fitted," she murmured to herself, hearing Starr's voice in her head. Her fingers landed on a deep emerald sweater dress she hadn't worn since last winter. It was soft, elegant, and hugged every curve just right. She held it up in front of the mirror, smiling at her reflection.

"Perfect," she whispered.

And as the city lights flickered through her window, she couldn't help but imagine what Marcus's face would look like when he saw her walk in wearing it.

CHAPTER 4
Christmas Eve Magic

MARCUS LAY in bed that night, the storm finally behind them, but his thoughts still spinning like snowflakes caught in the wind. No matter how many times he turned over, he kept seeing her face, the warmth in her smile, the way she said see you soon. He groaned, rubbing his hand over his chest. "Man, you don't even have her number," he muttered to himself. That thought alone was enough to get him out of bed. He grabbed his phone and scrolled through contacts before landing on one name, Reggie, his friend who owned a towing company.

"Yo," Reggie answered sleepily, "it's midnight, bro."

Marcus chuckled. "I owe you one, man. I need a favor, a big one. You remember that nurse I text you about, the one I helped on I-94? Her car's still out there."

"Say less," Reggie said with a yawn. "Send me the location. I'll grab it first thing in the morning."

"Appreciate you, bro."

When Marcus hung up, he sat back with a small, knowing smile. If she showed up tomorrow, he'd make sure her car was ready and running. And this time, he wouldn't let her leave without getting her number. That night, his dreams were a haze of green eyes, warm laughter, and snowflakes drifting around them like confetti. In one dream, she was in his arms, laughing as he brushed a snowflake from her cheek. He woke with his heart pounding and a smile that didn't fade all morning. By late afternoon on Christmas Eve, Mrs. Johnson's house was alive again. The scent of honey ham and sweet potato pie filled the air. Soulful Christmas music played softly in the background, and the tree sparkled like something out of a movie. Marcus had already been outside twice, checking the driveway where her car now sat clean, running, a brand-new battery under the hood. Every time headlights passed down the street, he found himself glancing toward the window.

Then he saw her.

A rideshare pulled up, and out stepped Jasmine wrapped in a long coat, but he caught a glimpse of an emerald, green dress beneath it. The dress hugged her in all the right places, her hair loose, her smile radiant. For a second, Marcus forgot how to breathe. When she walked in, Mrs. Johnson greeted her with open arms. "There's my snow angel! You made it, baby!"

"I told you I would," Jasmine said with a grin. Her eyes found Marcus's a moment later. "Hi, stranger."

"Hey yourself," he said softly, his voice low enough that only she could hear. "You look... incredible."

She blushed. "You clean up nice too." She loved his broad shoulders in the button down and the slacks left little to the imagination. Jasmine slowly licked her lips while taking him in from head to toe.

"Come on," he said, snapping her out of the fog and motioning her toward a window. "Got something to show you." When she saw her car parked in the driveway, her mouth fell open. "Marcus... you didn't."

He smiled. "Had a friend tow it early this morning. New battery, full tank, good as new."

"Marcus..." she said again, eyes wide with surprise and warmth. "You didn't have to do that."

"I wanted to," he said simply. "Couldn't let you worry about it during the holidays."

For a moment, she was quiet — the kind of quiet that said more than words ever could. Then she reached out, touching his cheek lightly. "Thank you. Really."

He kissed her palm before grabbing her hand to lead her to meet everyone. Dinner was full of laughter and good food. The house buzzed with joy, relatives swapping stories, friends singing along to Silent Night, Mrs. Johnson fussing over everyone's plates. Just as promised, she'd saved Jasmine a seat right next to Marcus. Halfway through the meal, their hands brushed under the table. Neither pulled away. The warmth of that touch lingered — soft, slow, deliberate. Then his fingers slid against hers again, intertwining. They didn't speak about it. Didn't need to. Every time their eyes met, they both smiled, secret smiles that held promises the night hadn't yet spoken. By the time dessert came around, Jasmine was full, from the food, the laughter, and something else entirely. She couldn't remember the last time she'd felt this welcomed, this... seen. After the plates were cleared, Marcus leaned in close, his breath brushing her ear. "You up for dessert and cocoa?"

She tilted her head, smiling. "Didn't we just have dessert?"

He grinned. "Not this kind, a special treat."

He stood, offering his hand. She followed him into the kitchen, where Mrs. Johnson's guests' laughter faded into the distance. The kitchen lights were soft and golden. On the counter sat a tray of untouched chocolate cake and two mugs waiting by the cocoa pot. Marcus handed her a mug, then nodded toward the back den — a quiet little corner lit by the glow of Christmas lights. They sat close, the silence between them warm and charged. Marcus took a slow sip, setting his cup down. His heartbeat beating hard in his chest.

"I've been waiting to ask you something," he said, his voice low, rough with honesty. "I never got your number. Figured I should fix that before you run off again."

Jasmine smiled, pulling her phone from her bag. "You're learning."

He laughed softly, taking her phone and typing in his contact. When he handed it back, their fingers brushed and neither pulled away.

"I should probably warn you," she said playfully, "I don't usually give out my number to men I meet during blizzards."

He leaned in slightly, his gaze holding hers. "Good thing I'm not just any man."

Their laughter faded into quiet again, the air thick with unspoken promise. Marcus's gaze dropped to her lips looking full, soft, and inviting. He hesitated, just long enough to see the answer already written in her eyes. Then he leaned in. The kiss was gentle at first — hesitant, testing then deeper, slower, the kind that made the rest of the world disappear. Her hand found his cheek, his fingers brushed her jaw, and for a moment, everything was still. Outside, snowflakes began to fall again light, peaceful, like the world was exhaling. When they finally pulled apart, Jasmine smiled, her voice barely a whisper. "Merry Christmas, Marcus."

He grinned, forehead resting against hers. "Best one I've ever had.

The party slowly wound down as the night deepened. The laughter faded to quiet conversation and soft Christmas tunes humming through the speakers. Mrs. Johnson's guests bundled up, hugging her at the door and exchanging "Merry Christmas" before disappearing into the gentle snowfall outside. Marcus and Jasmine found themselves still sitting together, two mugs of cocoa long gone, their conversation flowing like they'd known each other for years. They talked about everything, her hectic hospital shifts, his late nights at the plant, their favorite spots in the city, and childhood Christmas memories. Every time she laughed, Marcus felt something stir deeper, something that felt a lot like home. When the clock crept past midnight, Jasmine yawned softly, covering her mouth. "Sorry," she said, embarrassed. "Guess the food, the warmth, and the day all caught up to me."

Marcus smiled, his tone gentle. "No need to apologize. It's been a long couple of days."

Mrs. Johnson emerged from the kitchen carrying leftover containers. "Y'all head on out whenever you're ready. I'm about to turn in. Jasmine, baby, you sure you don't want to stay the night again?"

Jasmine smiled warmly. "You've been too kind already. I don't want to overstay my welcome."

Before Mrs. Johnson could insist again, Marcus spoke up. "I'll drive her home. Her car's running fine now, and I can just Uber back."

Jasmine hesitated, biting her lip. "You don't have to do that, Marcus. I'll be okay."

He chuckled softly. "You really think I'm letting you drive home this late after everything? Not happening."

Her heart tugged a little at the protectiveness in his tone. "You're relentless, you know that?"

He grinned. "So, I've been told."

She finally sighed. "All right, fine. But you're bringing my car back tomorrow for breakfast."

"Deal," he said, eyes glinting.

They stepped outside into the crisp night. Snow had started falling again soft and steady, catching the glow of the streetlights. The drive was quiet at first, filled with low Christmas music and the occasional hum of the heater. Jasmine kept sneaking glances at him the way his jaw flexed as he drove, the faint smile that never seemed to fade.

"You sure you're okay driving back in this?" she asked as they neared her building.

"I'll be fine," he said easily. "Grew up driving in worse."

But when they pulled into her complex, the snow had

thickened, falling in heavy, steady sheets. Jasmine frowned, looking out the windshield. "It's really coming down again." Marcus parked, glancing toward the sky. "Looks like round two." She turned to him, chewing her lip for a second before speaking softly. "You should stay. The roads are getting bad again, and I'd feel awful if something happened to you."

He looked at her, surprised — not by the offer, but by how much he wanted to say yes. "You sure?"

She nodded. "I've got a couch, extra blankets, and you've already saved me once. Seems only fair."

He smiled. "All right. But I'm taking the couch, and that's final."

Inside, her apartment was cozy and softly lit was a small tree glowing in the corner, stocking hanging by the wall. She handed him a blanket and pointed toward the couch. "You can crash here. I'll grab pillows." As she moved around the living room, Marcus looked around and everything about her space felt like her. Warm. Peaceful. Real. Once the pillows were set, she turned on the TV, flipping to a holiday movie marathon. "You can't stay over and not watch holiday classics," she said with a smile.

"Which one?" he asked.

She smirked. "The Preacher's Wife. It's my tradition."

He laughed. "Denzel and Whitney? I can't argue with that."

They settled in, her on one end of the couch, him on the other. But as the movie went on, the space between them somehow disappeared. They talked, joked, and shared stories about childhood holidays until the conversation turned into soft laughter and quiet sighs. At some point, Jasmine's head rested against the pillow, her eyes fluttering closed. Marcus felt his own lids grow heavy too, but when he stirred an hour later, he realized she had fallen asleep beside him peacefully, and her breathing steady. He shifted slightly, meaning to grab the blanket, but paused. Another holiday movie flickering softly on the screen, lighting her face in a warm glow. She looked like something out of a dream. Carefully, he reached for the blanket and draped it over her. She stirred, eyes half-open, her voice soft and sleepy. "Marcus?"

"Yeah," he whispered. "Go back to sleep. You're good."

He tucked the blanket around her shoulders. When he leaned closer, she smiled, eyes still heavy with sleep. "You're sweet," she murmured.

Without thinking, he brushed a stray curl from her forehead and pressed a gentle kiss there. "Merry Christmas, Jasmine."

She blinked slowly, her smile deepening. Then, before he could pull back, she reached up — her hand warm against his neck and drew him down for a kiss. It started soft, hesitant, but deepened quickly, slow, sweet, full of the emotion they'd both been holding back since that night at his moms. When they finally broke apart, she whispered against his lips, "Merry Christmas, Marcus." He smiled, resting his forehead against hers as the snow fell outside and It's a Wonderful Life played quietly in the background. In that moment, with the city hushed under fresh snow and her heartbeat echoing softly against his chest, Marcus knew this Christmas would be one he'd never forget.

CHAPTER 5

Christmas Morning

THE FIRST LIGHT of Christmas morning crept through Jasmine's blinds, soft and golden. The snow outside had finally stopped, blanketing Detroit in a shimmering stillness that made everything look touched by magic. Marcus stirred first, blinking against the sunlight. For a moment, he didn't know where he was until he saw the twinkling Christmas lights, the small tree in the corner, and Jasmine still curled up beside him, wrapped in the blanket they'd shared. She looked peaceful, her lips parted in a faint smile, a loose curl falling across her face. He smiled to himself, remembering the warmth of their kiss and the way she'd whispered Merry Christmas last night like it was a promise. He moved carefully, not wanting to wake her, and slipped into the kitchen. The cupboards creaked softly as he searched through them, finding pancake mix, eggs, bacon, and a half-full bottle of vanilla extract.

"Perfect," he murmured.

A few minutes later, the smell of breakfast filled the air, buttery pancakes sizzling, bacon crisping, and coffee brewing. He'd just flipped another pancake when he heard a sleepy voice behind him.

"So, you're just gonna make breakfast in my kitchen without supervision?"

He turned, grinning. Jasmine leaned against the doorway, still wrapped in the blanket, hair tousled and smile soft. "Morning," he said.

She laughed quietly. "Morning. You trying to outdo Santa?"

"Maybe," he said, flipping a pancake onto the stack. "Figured I'd earn another Christmas invite."

"You didn't need to," she said, walking over to the counter. "You already did."

Their eyes met, lingering for a moment longer than either planned. Then Jasmine reached for two mugs, pouring coffee while he plated the food. The small kitchen filled with the easy rhythm of them moving together, passing utensils, bumping elbows, laughing when the bacon popped too close to her hand.

"You're surprisingly domestic," she teased.

He chuckled. "My mom raised me right. Plus, I learned quick that if I want a good breakfast, I better know how to make it." They sat down at her small table by the window, steam rising from their plates. Outside, the city glowed, sunlight bouncing off snowdrifts, kids' laughter echoing from somewhere down the block.

"This feels nice," Jasmine said after a while, sipping her coffee. "Peaceful."

"Yeah," he said quietly. "It does."

They talked between bites about childhood Christmases, about how neither of them had expected their holiday to turn out like this.

"You know," she said with a playful smile, "a blizzard, a tow truck, and a man who cooks breakfast in my kitchen. Sounds like a Hallmark movie."

He laughed. "Yeah? What would you call it?"

She thought for a second, pretending to consider. "Hmm. Snowed In on I-94."

He chuckled, shaking his head. "I like that."

When their laughter faded, silence settled again — not awkward, but intimate. Marcus reached across the table, brushing his thumb over her hand. "So... what happens after the credits roll, Jasmine?" She smiled, eyes glinting in the morning light. "I guess we find out."

He leaned closer, his voice low. "I'd like that."

Before he could say anything else, she slid her hand into his, intertwining their fingers just like they had under the dinner table the night before.

"Merry Christmas, Marcus," she whispered again, her tone full of warmth.

He smiled, squeezing her hand. "Merry Christmas, Jasmine."

And this time, neither of them was in any hurry to leave.

CHAPTER 6
Winter Promises

SINCE THAT UNFORGETTABLE Christmas morning they had been inseparable going to dinners, him driving her to work and picking her up. If they weren't together, they were talking on the phone or texting each other. Detroit was still blanketed in snow, the streets lined with frost and twinkling lights that refused to come down even after the holiday. But for Jasmine, the cold didn't bite the same way anymore. Not since Marcus. Every day since Christmas, he'd texted or called — little check-ins that made her smile no matter how chaotic her shifts got. You eat yet? How's my favorite nurse? Don't make me come up there with soup. Their nights filled with laughter, long talks, and a growing sense of something real, something steady. Saturday, the city was wrapped in silver lights. Jasmine had just finished her shift at the hospital and was tugging on her coat when her phone buzzed.

Marcus: I'm outside. Thought you might need a ride home.

She smiled at the screen, shaking her head. You know I can drive, right?

Marcus: Yeah, but then I'd miss an excuse to see you and don't act like you don't like being a passenger princess.

Rolling her eyes fondly, she typed back, Give me five minutes, hero. When she stepped outside, the air was crisp and her breath puffed out like smoke. Marcus stood by his truck, leaning against it in that effortless way that made her heartbeat skip. He wore a thick black peacoat, his breath visible as he smiled.

"Hey, Nurse Jasmine," he said. "Rough shift?"

She sighed, climbing into the truck. "Full moon. ER was chaos. But I made it."

He started the engine, heater humming to life. "Good. I've got plans to make it better."

"Oh yeah?" she teased, arching a brow. "What kind of plans?"

He smirked. "You'll see."

He drove them downtown, where Campus Martius was lit up like a postcard. The big Christmas tree still standing tall, the skating rink glowing beneath fairy lights. Families and couples skating hand in hand, and laughter echoing through the cold air.

Jasmine looked out the window in awe. "You're kidding. You brought me ice skating?"

"Absolutely," he said, already getting out. "Figured you should have a proper winter experience minus the blizzard this time and because I saw how that scene in The Preachers Wife made you light up."

She laughed. "You do realize nurses aren't built for falling on ice, right? Plus, I am not Whitney!"

He walked around to open her door, offering his hand. "Good thing you've got an engineer that's good with his hands to catch you."

She took his hand, stepping out into the glow of the city lights. Her heart fluttered at the warmth of his touch — familiar now, but no less electric. They skated or at least tried to. Jasmine clung to his arm, laughing every few seconds as she slipped. Marcus didn't let go once. Every stumble brought her closer to him; every laugh made him fall for her a little more. When she finally found her balance, she looked up at him, cheeks flushed, eyes sparkling. "Okay," she said between giggles, "maybe this isn't so bad."

"Told you." He murmured, brushing a strand of hair from her face. "You just needed the right partner."

They circled the rink again, hand in hand, the city lights reflecting in the ice. When the cold finally got to them, Marcus led her off the rink and toward a nearby café glowing with warmth and steam-frosted windows. They sat by the window with cocoa and shared a slice of red velvet cake, the world outside glittering like a dream. "Funny," Jasmine said softly. "I was stranded on I-94, thinking the world was ending. Now I can't imagine it without you."

Marcus's hand found hers across the table, his thumb tracing slow circles over her skin. "That's the thing about storms," he said quietly. "Sometimes they don't come to destroy — they come to clear the path."

Her heart melted.

He reached into his coat pocket, pulling out a small, wrapped box. "Might be a little late for Christmas," he said, sliding it toward her, "but I wanted you to have this." Inside was a simple silver bracelet, delicate, with a small snowflake charm that caught the light.

"Marcus..." she whispered, touched. "It's beautiful."

He smiled, eyes soft. "Just a reminder that even the coldest nights can bring something worth keeping." She leaned over the table, cupping his face in her hands, and kissed him slowly and deep, the world outside fading again into quiet snow. When they finally pulled apart, she nipped his lip and whispered, "You're something else, Marcus."

He grinned. "Nah. I'm just a guy lucky enough to get snowed in with the right woman."

Outside, snow began to fall again — light, peaceful, endless. But this time, it didn't feel like a storm. It felt like a beginning.

CHAPTER 7

Fireworks and Forever

THE NEW YEAR was days away, and Detroit was still shimmering beneath the weight of winter. The city buzzed with post-holiday life, lights still hanging in windows, snow piled high along the curbs. But for Jasmine, life felt lighter, brighter. Marcus had become the warmth she hadn't realized she was missing. They'd spent nearly every day together since meeting each other — dinners, movie nights, long talks that stretched into dawn. So, when Marcus showed up at her apartment one cold afternoon, eyes sparkling with mischief, she knew something was up.

"Why do you look like you're about to get me in trouble?" she asked, crossing her arms.

He grinned and held up an envelope. "Because I probably am. I need you to do me one favor."

She tilted her head. "What's that?"

"Take off."

"Marcus—" she started to protest, but he cut her off with that smooth confidence that always disarmed her.

"Before you say no, just trust me. I already checked — you've got the vacation days. I called your friend Starr to make sure she'd cover your shift."

Her mouth fell open. "You what?"

He chuckled. "I said I'd make it up to her with two spa days at the resort we're going to."

"Resort?" she repeated, blinking. "What resort?"

He stepped closer, his voice dropping low. "Boyne Mountain. A couple days, maybe a week. Snow, fires, dinners, just you and me."

Her heart fluttered. "Marcus... that's—"

He grinned. "A, yes?"

She laughed, shaking her head. "You don't even give a girl time to say no."

"Good, Lets Go" he said, slipping his arms around her waist. "I didn't want you to."

Welcome to Boyne Mountain Resort the sign read. The drive up north was like something out of a postcard. Snow-capped trees lined the winding roads, and every turn revealed a stretch of white hills glistening under the winter sun. When they arrived at the resort, Jasmine's eyes went wide — cozy log cabins with smoke curling from chimneys, the scent of pine in the air, and people bundled in bright scarves walking toward the slopes.

"This is incredible," she breathed.

Marcus smiled, grabbing their bags. "Only the best for my favorite nurse."

This was straight out of a winter dream. They spent mornings skiing and tubing down the hills, laughter echoing through the crisp air. Afternoons meant couples massages, cocoa by the fire, and quiet walks beneath the trees as snowflakes drifted down like whispers. At night, Marcus spoiled her with candlelit dinners — wine, slow music, and the kind of soft glances that said more than words ever could. Each evening ended the same way: curled up together by the fireplace, her head resting on his chest, the world outside fading to white. By the time New Year's Eve arrived, Jasmine couldn't imagine life without him. That evening, Marcus told her to dress warmly but didn't say why. She laughed as he tugged her hand, leading her outside into the night. The resort glittered with lights, music drifting from the main lodge. Snow fell gently, catching in her curls.

"Marcus, where are we going?" she asked, half laughing, half shivering.

He grinned, tightening his hold on her hand. "You'll see."

When they reached the top of the ski hill, she gasped. There, under a glowing canopy of fairy lights, stood a small crowd — Mrs. Johnson, Starr, Jasmine's family, and a few close friends, all smiling.

Her hand flew to her mouth. "Marcus... what is this?"

He turned to face her, snow crunching beneath his boots. "You once told me you never expected that blizzard on I-94 — that it was the worst day of your year. But for me, it was the best one of my life."

Her eyes filled with tears as he dropped to one knee, pulling a small velvet box from his pocket. "Jasmine Carter, you changed my world. You made me believe in peace, in timing, in love showing up right when you least expect it. I don't want another new year without you. Will you marry me?" Tears spilled down her cheeks as she nodded, speechless. "Yes," she whispered, laughing through her tears. "Yes, Marcus, a thousand times yes." Then, to her utter shock, Mrs. Johnson stepped forward, holding a bouquet. "Well, what are we waiting for?" she said, beaming. "We got the minister right here."

Jasmine blinked, laughing in disbelief. "You planned this?"

Marcus smiled, slipping the ring onto her finger. "Every detail."

"Tonight?" she asked breathlessly. "We're getting married tonight?"

He nodded. "Right here. Right now. When the clock strikes midnight."

As the countdown began below ten, nine, eight — Marcus took her hands in his, eyes, never leaving hers.

"Seven, six, five..."

The crowd chanted louder, fireworks waiting.

"Four, three..."

Her heart raced.

"Two, one—"

The sky exploded in color as the clock struck twelve. Marcus leaned forward, whispering, "Happy New Year, Mrs. Johnson," as he kissed her deeply cheers erupted as fireworks burst and danced across the sky — gold, silver, and crimson streaks lighting up the snow. Snowflakes drifted down as they exchanged vows right there on the hill — simple, heartfelt, perfect. Surrounded by the people they loved, wrapped in the glow of new beginnings, Jasmine realized that sometimes, love really did write its own story and when you know you know. Some may say it was fast but the chemistry they shared was surreal and she knew her soul belonged to him.

And their story began in the middle of a storm — only to end under fireworks and forever.

CHAPTER 8

Epilogue

ONE YEAR LATER

THE WIND WAS SOFTER this time. Snow still dusted the slopes at Boyne Mountain, but the air carried a gentler chill — the kind that whispered of love rather than storms.

Jasmine stepped out of the cabin, bundled in a long cream coat and matching gloves. The familiar sight of the glowing lodge and distant laughter from the ski hill made her heart swell. A year ago, she'd stood on that very hilltop, heart pounding, as fireworks painted the sky and Marcus slipped a ring onto her finger. Now, that ring glimmered in the sunlight as she reached up to adjust her scarf.

"Déjà vu?" came the deep, familiar voice behind her.

She turned and smiled as Marcus walked up, snow crunching under his boots, carrying two steaming cups of cocoa. "A little," she said, taking one. "Except this time, I'm not in shock."

He laughed, wrapping an arm around her waist. "Last year was a winter wonderland. This year we are basking in our love."

"I feel so at peace," she echoed, leaning into him. "And a whole lot of love."

They walked together toward the overlook where they'd

said their vows. The hill was empty now, quiet except for the rustle of wind through the pines. Marcus stopped, setting his cocoa down in the snow, and turned to face her fully.

"You know," he said softly, "I'll never forget that night. You in that dress, snow in your hair, fireworks lighting up your smile."

She blushed, laughing gently. "And you calling me Mrs. Johnson."

He grinned. "Best decision I ever made."

She tilted her head. "Oh yeah? Even better than rescuing a stranded nurse on I-94?" He chuckled. "That's where it started. But what we built after... that's the blessing." He pulled her closer, their breaths mingling in the crisp air.

"And speaking of blessings..." she said.

From her coat pocket, she pulled out a small, wrapped box.

His eyes widened. "Jasmine... what is this?"

She handed it to him, the corners of her mouth curving in that soft smile he'd fallen for.

"Go ahead, open it baby." she said.

He peeled the wrapping carefully, revealing a tiny pair of white baby booties tied together with a gold ribbon.

His lips parted, eyes glistening as he looked up at him. "Baby... A BABY"

She smiled, eyes full of quiet joy. "Guess we're not the only Johnsons coming back here next year." Tears filled their eyes, and she laughed through them, covering her mouth. "YES! We're having a baby!"

He nodded, cupping her face in his hands. "Our little winter miracle."

Jasmine threw her arms around him, laughing, crying, holding on tight. The snow swirled around them, the world shimmering in soft white and silver.

When she finally looked up, she whispered, "You always know how to make a girl fall in love with winter."

He kissed her forehead gently. "You made me love every season."

As the sun dipped behind the mountains and the sky turned pink with the promise of a beautiful future.

They stood hand in hand, hearts full, watching the sunset and the skies color reflect off the snow.

One year ago, a storm had brought them together and gave them forever — and now with something even greater on the way.

The End

"Sometimes the coldest nights lead you straight to the warmest hearts."

Let's Connect

Thank you for reading! If you enjoyed this book, please consider leaving a review on Goodreads, Amazon, or StoryGraph.

For merch, updates, and more about my work, visit my official site:

LinkedIn: Author Shani Denise
TikTok: @authorbydayreaderbynite
Facebook: @Author Shani Denise
Instagram/Threads: @authorbydayreaderbynite

Also by Shani Denise

Summertime in the City

Peaches wasn't looking for love when she came home to Detroit—she was chasing peace, hiding from heartbreak, and trying to find herself between block parties and steamy summer nights. But then Que rolled up in that candy-painted Impala, tattoos gleaming, eyes full of fire, and a past as complicated as hers.

He's the kind of man your mama warns you about—but your soul leans into.

She's the kind of woman he didn't see coming—but now can't let go.

As city heat rises, so do their feelings—slow kisses on porch steps, secret studio nights, and heart-to-hearts in the backseat. But when summer starts slipping away, so does the illusion that love will be enough. Life pulls them in opposite directions, testing whether this was a summer fling... or the start of forever.

One city. One summer. One unforgettable love.

Also by Shani Denise

When The City Sleeps

Nia never meant to fall for him.

Darius — known on the streets as D — was everything she promised herself to stay away from: powerful, dangerous, too tied to the world she swore she'd never get pulled into. But late nights in Detroit have a way of bringing strangers together, and when she crosses paths with Darius, she's caught between fear and fascination. One chance encounter, one spark too strong to ignore, and suddenly Nia finds herself drawn into his orbit. What begins as stolen glances and heat-laced words burns into something deeper — something raw, tender, and unstoppable. Darius finds in Nia the peace he didn't know he needed, a reason to step out of the shadows and start building a different future.

But the streets don't let go easy.

When old rivals bring danger too close to home, Nia forces Darius to choose between being D — the man everyone fears — or Darius, the man she's learning to love. And walking away from the life he built could cost them both everything.

One city. One love. One chance to prove that even in the dead of night, their hearts can still find forever.

Also by Shani Denise

Kissed By Chaos

In Detroit, love isn't just powerful—it's dangerous.

Krystina hides the fire burning beneath her skin, afraid of what happens when her emotions ignite. Dre hides behind his chain and hood, but his glowing red eyes betray the truth: he can read the thoughts people try to bury.

When they meet, sparks become wildfire. Their connection awakens a forgotten bloodline—one where power is inherited through love, and fear feeds the darkness stalking them.

As shadows close in, Dre and Krystina must face their deepest truth: the chaos hunting them isn't a curse from outside. It's born from their fear... and only their love can stop it.

A supernatural love story about fire, fate, and the magic hidden in the heart of Detroit.

Also by Shani Denise

Home for the Holidays

When celebrity makeup artist Tiera Davis returns home for Thanksgiving after nearly three years away, she expects awkward family dinners — not him answering the door. Shawn Reed, her childhood best friend and ex-boyfriend, has become part of her family's world in her absence. Torn between pride and the comfort she left behind, Tiera must face old wounds, buried love, and the question she's avoided for years: Can you ever really come home — if the heart you left behind is still waiting on the porch?

www.ingramcontent.com/pod-product-compliance
Lightning Source LLC
La Vergne TN
LVHW010943110826
845149LV00013B/2743

* 9 7 9 8 9 9 9 7 0 5 9 5 2 *